My Dog, CAT

My Dog, CAT

by **Marty Crisp**

illustrated by **True Kelley**

SCHOLASTIC INC.

New York   Toronto   London   Auckland   Sydney
Mexico City   New Delhi   Hong Kong   Buenos Aires

To Jessamyn, my Yorkie,
And to all the other flesh-and-blood dogs
I've loved over the years:
Inky, Sammy, Paddy,
Mandy, Pooh, Max, Spike,
Fozzie, and Molly
M.C.

ISBN 0-439-36848-0

12 11 10 9 8 7 6 5 4 3 2   2 3 4 5 6 7/0

Printed in the U.S.A.   40

First Scholastic printing, March 2002

Contents

I. Runtface

There are dog people.

And there are cat people.

Abbott Williamson the Third figured he was a dog person living in a cat people family.

His mother had a gray, short-haired tabby cat. His father had a big yellow tomcat with a white belly. His sister had a calico longhair who constantly shed tufts of fur on Abbie's jeans and sweatshirts and, if he didn't keep his bedroom door closed, even on his pillow.

Usually, Abbie didn't like cats. But right now, right this very minute, he wished he had a cat beside him.

Not a house cat.

A lion. The King of Beasts.

Even a tiger would do, as long as it was big and loud and hungry. Hungry enough to eat Pete Street right out of his sneakers.

Abbie looked down at those scuffed sneakers. It was better than looking up at Pete's challenging eyes.

"Wazzup, Runtface?" Pete and his friends Jeff and Jason were crowded around Abbie's open locker, waiting to get their mitts on his lunch.

Pete always wanted Abbie's dessert. Most days, he got it before school, ambushing Abbie on his way through the park. Pete would have his shaggy, black-and-tan Akita with him. Tiny was the dog's name, although it was huge. As far as Abbie was concerned, the dog was big and mean and squinty-eyed, just like her owner. Tiny would snarl and growl and act as if she didn't mind if Pete ate Abbie's dessert, as long as she herself could chew on Abbie.

But this morning, Pete was running a little late.

"I'll get my lunch bag." Abbie knew better than to argue with a giant. Pete Street wasn't just tall, he towered over Abbie. And he

seemed to enjoy towering over him. It wasn't fair. After you moved into a new school, it took a while to meet the nice kids, but the mean kids zoned in on you as if they had geek radar. As if they knew you were coming.

Abbie stood on his toes and felt around on the top shelf of his locker, where he'd shoved his lunch bag out of sight just minutes earlier. If only he'd get his growth spurt right this minute. His mother kept promising he'd grow into his big feet someday. Abbie glanced down at his black high-tops. Why not today? He could almost picture it. He stared for a moment at his sneakers, trying to imagine them on the end of the legs of the tallest basketball center in the world.

He'd be tall, all right. And he'd still be growing. His head would zoom toward the ceiling, and he'd stick his tongue out at Pete as he shot past. There'd be nothing Pete could do about it. That's what Abbie wished for.

Wishing was sort of his hobby. He collected wishes the way other kids collected comic books and baseball cards. He dreamed of finding a magic coin or a genie's lamp or bumping into a fairy godmother. Fairy godmothers were for girls, of course, but since he had a girl's name, who knew? The wishes came to him, and he stored them in his memory, to take out and examine and decide if they were what he really, really wanted.

Back in Baltimore, he'd sometimes come close to wasting wishes on dumb things like second helpings of cake or not having to take a bath.

Not anymore. He'd been refining his list, ever since they moved here.

There were strict rules for wishes. You could never have more than three, no matter what kind of magic you used. These days, Abbie knew exactly what he wanted.

First, he'd wish for another name. Any other name. Matt or Josh or Joe. Anything that didn't sound like a girl's name. How the Williamson family could give such a horrible name to three generations of boys was beyond Abbie. Of course his dad, who was Abbott Williamson Junior, used a nickname: Will. Before that, it went back to his grandfather. Abbie had no idea how he'd handled being stuck with a girl's name. Maybe names hadn't mattered so much in the olden days.

Abbie pulled his lunch bag down from his locker shelf. He handed it to Pete without a word. He was tempted to wish Pete Street would disappear in a big puff of black smoke. Magic disappearing smoke. Abbie figured it would smell slightly of burnt toast, the way Pete did.

But that would be a wasted wish. There were plenty of bullies in the world. Getting rid of one was no protection in the long run.

Better to wish to be taller. Taller than any other boy in the fourth grade. Big enough to make Pete and every other bully think twice about messing with Abbott Williamson the Third.

Abbie stood on his toes again to search the back of his locker shelf for his library book. It was due today.

It was a book about dogs. That, of course, would be his third wish: to have a dog of his own. A big, strong, black dog named Killer. Maybe a Rottweiler or a Doberman pinscher. It didn't really matter, as long as the dog was

Runtface

huge and fierce and had teeth the size of piano keys. It had to be a dog who would follow him everywhere and make bullies take off their baseball caps, nod their heads respectfully, and murmur "Wazzup, Abbie."

"So, wazzup, Runtface?" Pete tossed Abbie's lunch bag to Jeff, who in turn tossed it to Jason. Jeff and Jason were also fourth graders, and not much smaller than Pete himself. They followed Pete everywhere. Pete was stocky with close-cropped brown hair and a knotted blue bandana always hanging out of his back pocket. He carried his valuables in the bandana instead of a wallet. Abbie had seen him taking money out of it.

Jason tossed the bag back to Pete, who withdrew the plastic pie-slice container, licked a dribble of whipped cream off the corner of the lid, and flipped it open. He ate a big fingerful of strawberry pie, slurping it around on his tongue and licking his lips. Then he scrunched up the brown paper bag so Abbie's peanut-butter-and-jelly sandwich was smushed and his banana was half popped out of its skin.

7

"Wazzup?" Pete prodded. He used this to cover every occasion, from "hello" to "get lost." A greeting to a friend also included a high five and a hip bump.

Abbie definitely was not a friend.

"I hope you enjoy my pie, Pete. I'll try to bring something even better next time."

Abbie had learned the hard way, with what seemed like a million pounds of bully sitting on his chest, that this was what Pete wanted to hear. Abbie's voice sounded flat and faraway as he said the words. He hated to say them. But if he said them all sarcastic and bitter—the way he felt—Pete would just sit on his chest again until he did it right.

"You do that, Runtface. You go home to your mommy and ask her to bake up some of her chocolate chip cookies," Pete suggested, patting Abbie on the head as if he were a little kindergartner.

"She might be baking today." Abbie hoped the gleam of revenge he felt rising in his eyes wasn't visible. He pushed his gold wire-rimmed glasses up his nose and tilted his head toward the overhead fluorescent lights. He hoped all Pete could see was a reflected glare. "We're having company this weekend. My aunt is coming over and bringing her new baby, and Mom usually bakes when we're having company."

"Well, isn't that sweet?" Pete made a mincing gesture with his free hand, and the other boys hooted with laughter.

"Get to class," came the warning voice of the hall monitor as she turned the corner. "It's almost time for the bell."

"Just be sure to bring something good," Pete growled, putting his lips to Abbie's ear. "You getting the message, Runtface?"

Abbie could smell the bully's breath, ripe with cornflakes and Abbie's own strawberry pie.

"Sure, Pete. I'll bring something good, just for you. It'll be a surprise. I promise." Abbie tried hard to sound sincere. Humble, even. He didn't want to scare Pete. Not yet. There'd be time enough for that later. Soon Abbie would have his dog, and everything would be different.

The back of Abbie's neck tingled with anticipation. Tonight was the night one of his three wishes would finally come true, even if it was temporary. Aunt Laura was bringing her new baby over, and with him, she was bringing her new dog.

She'd refused to tell Abbie what kind of a dog it was. She wanted to surprise him. All she would say was that her dog could bark a warning and sniff out trouble with the best of them.

Now she wanted the Williamson family to dog-sit while she flew off and showed baby Lee to relatives in California.

Abbie could picture it already: a big black dog trotting at his side. A dog whose deep, menacing growl would light a flame of fear in Pete Street's eyes the next time he tried messing with Abbott Williamson the Third.

2. A Dog Named Cat

How could he have known? How could he possibly have known Aunt Laura was a lunatic?

He'd always thought his mother's younger sister was cool for an adult. She played softball, and she could actually hit. She was awesome at taking down the bad guys in Abbie's Dragon Attack video game. But when it came to dogs, apparently Aunt Laura didn't have a clue.

Abbie sighed and shook his head for the fifty-seventh time. Aunt Laura's "guard dog" was a surprise, all right, and the surprise was all his. Sure, Aunt Laura had never said what kind of dog she'd gotten. But a dog was a dog. How bad could it be?

Poodles might look sissified, but they had strong teeth and claws. Dalmatians barked a lot, but they weren't afraid of anything. Even a dumpy little bulldog could clamp on to the seat of Pete Street's pants as he stood with his feet apart and his hands on his hips, showing off on the playground. A bulldog could hang on forever. Or at least as long as it took Pete to beg for mercy.

But Abbie *never* expected the creature Aunt Laura placed in his stiff, unwilling arms. He hadn't known an animal could weigh less than a bag of dog food and still be called a dog.

"I got the puppy almost full grown so he'd be easier to train," Aunt Laura told Abbie. Aunt Laura's baby, little Lee, pulled cheerfully on his mother's long, shiny blond hair. Abbie's favorite aunt had hair exactly the same color as his own, only hers was way past her shoulders and his was so short it hardly ever needed combing. Abbie had always felt close to Aunt Laura. But how could you feel close to a relative who went and did something like this?

Abbie wasn't sure he could ever forgive her.

Aunt Laura babbled on, clearly unaware of Abbie's unhappiness. "I wanted to get a dog that was just the right size for Lee. A Yorkshire terrier was perfect. And, of course, I couldn't resist giving him a literary name. It appealed to me as a student of history."

She was referring, of course, to the midget dog's totally ridiculous name. Abbie could feel a small squirm of sympathy stirring in his belly as he looked at the steel-blue dog with the tiny dark eyes and the tousled tan head.

"I named him after the Roman lyric poet Catullus," continued Aunt Laura. "I listed the name on his American Kennel Club papers as Catullus the Great. I figured, what could be cuter than a dog named Cat?"

"Cat?" Abbie's voice squeaked as he said the word.

Aunt Laura grinned cheerfully. "Don't you love the name, Abbie? Isn't it cute?"

"It's . . ." Abbie started to blurt out exactly what he was thinking. He wanted to shout, "It's a stupid name. It's like having a 'Kick Me' sign taped to your back." But he caught the warning look in his mother's eye.

"It's okay," he mumbled.

Aunt Laura went right on talking to his mother. "This dog is such a sweetheart, Sharon. I'd pack him up and take him along on the plane, but Jerry insists we're going to have our hands full, traveling with Lee."

"Don't worry about a thing." Abbie's mother scooped the soft-furred creature out of her son's unresisting grip, ruffled its coat, and gave it back to Abbie. She gave him another warning look at the same time. "Abbie has been wanting a dog for years. This will be a great opportunity for him to see if dogs are as much fun as he thinks. So stop worrying."

Abbie lifted the dog from his lap and put it on the floor. That was a weird thing for his mother to say. His mom knew better than anybody what kind of dog he'd been wishing for. He'd talked about it nonstop since Aunt Laura called to say she was bringing her new dog.

"You're sure six weeks won't be too long?" Aunt Laura sounded doubtful. "I would have waited to get a dog if I'd known we were going to get this chance to go see Jerry's folks. It's just that Yorkies are so precious. You know what they say. Good things come in small packages."

Aunt Laura winked at Abbie.

He wished she hadn't. It felt like she was secretly telling him he was a small package, too. "If you have any trouble, Shar," Aunt Laura continued, "please go ahead and put Cat in a kennel. Have them send the bill to us."

"You worry too much, Laura." Abbie's mom was leading her sister toward the front door. "Abbie's had to be content with cats all these years. So it's perfect for him to start out here with a dog named Cat."

The house was filled with the lingering aroma of freshly baked chocolate chip cookies, but for once, the smell didn't make Abbie's mouth water. In fact, he doubted he could choke down a single cookie past the lump in his throat.

Perfect was not a word he'd ever use to describe Cat.

"You go on out to California. Don't give it another thought."

A Dog Named Cat

But Abbie gave it another thought. In fact, it was all he could think about. This dog could never be a bodyguard. This dog looked as if it *needed* a bodyguard.

Somehow the Yorkie had found its way into Abbie's lap again. Its front paws rested on his sweatshirt. It poked curiously around his chin with its cold black nose and began to lick his cheeks and the insides of his ears. It kept licking until its tickling tongue was on his nose, smudging his glasses.

Abbie grabbed the Yorkie and set it back on the floor, holding it there firmly. The little piece of fur seemed to like him. But he didn't return the feeling.

When Abbie let go of the dog, Cat picked up a sock where Abbie had dropped it after school. Cat began to shake it as if it were some kind of vanquished game and he a mighty wolf.

"You have a better imagination than I do," Abbie told Cat as he cleaned his smudged glasses. While he was wiping them, the little dog jumped back into his lap, the sock dangling from his mouth.

Abbie sighed.

MY DOG, CAT

Maybe his mom or dad, or even his sister, Marie, would take the mutt off his hands. Talk about not getting your wish. Of all possible dogs in the whole world, Cat was absolutely the last dog Abbie would ever wish for.

3. A Dog by Any Other Name

"I want a kitten. Dogs smell," insisted Marie.

Marie was Abbie's five-year-old sister. She wasn't likely to take over the care and feeding of a dog. She was too busy holding make-believe tea parties with her Giggletime Gloria doll and brushing her stupid old calico until it was a wonder the animal had any hair left to shed.

Abbie's mom didn't seem to know what to make of Cat. The only thing certain was that she considered him Abbie's responsibility. There was no doubt in Abbie's mind that if she ever felt she had to take over the little dog's care, it would only be after a lot of yelling about how he'd promised to do this favor for Aunt Laura and wasn't doing it.

He *was* doing it, of course. He couldn't very well let a dog starve, and Abbie figured it would probably only take missing one meal for this peanut-size canine to go under.

Why would anybody want such an un-doglike dog?

Aunt Laura had told them L. Frank Baum had written *The Wizard of Oz* with Toto as a Yorkie, just like Cat. But Hollywood picked a cairn terrier to play the part in the movie, not a Yorkie.

A Yorkie was too small. A Yorkie could never be a star. It could never be a dog named Killer, either. Abbie only wished, if he had to be stuck with an animal named Cat, it could at least be a big black panther.

The Yorkie trotted behind Abbie to the kitchen table, sitting at his feet when he plopped in his chair and reached for the milk. Abbie's dad looked up from his morning oatmeal and the sports section of the newspaper and winked.

"So! Looks like we got ourselves a new dog,"

offered Abbie's father conversationally. "How did you two get along last night?"

Marie, who was almost through with breakfast, stuffed a final bite of banana in her mouth and flounced out of the room, snorting in disgust.

"I wanted a kitten," she repeated, but she had so much banana in her mouth, it sounded to Abbie more like, "Iva akit."

"We don't need any more cats," their dad called after her, somehow understanding Marie despite the banana. Abbie couldn't agree more. He could never even remember the names of the cats they already had. They didn't come when you called, after all. It just wasn't worth the effort.

The big yellow tom rubbed against his dad's ankles, ignoring Cat completely. "That little pup isn't much bigger than a kitten, is it? Hard to believe it's full grown. Abbie, why don't you take him for a walk around the block?" he suggested. "Let him stretch his legs."

"The backyard is big enough." Abbie didn't bother to explain that he didn't want to be seen with such a tiny dog. He could just hear

A Dog by Any Other Name

Pete Street: "Runtface Williamson and his runtface dog." And there'd be no defense, of course. No bodyguard. The most this dog could guard was a big toe.

The big yellow tom paraded past the kitchen table. Cat barked with excitement and tried to follow, but Abbie hooked a finger through the little dog's collar, stopping him.

The tom hissed in Cat's direction.

Cat huddled close, rubbing against the leg of Abbie's jeans.

Catullus the Great? No way.

More like Catullus the Not-So-Great.

4. A Cat Is Not a Kitty

Marie was the first one to give in.

Everybody played with the dog. Laughed at the dog. Petted the dog. But Abbie was pretty sure no one in the family really *liked* the dog.

Abbie fed Cat. His mother gave the dog baths. His father put boards over the cellar window wells so Cat wouldn't fall in.

But it was Marie who began taking Cat up to her room and dressing the patient Yorkie in a dishrag cape, a rhinestone bracelet crown, and a variety of hand-me-down clothes from her Giggletime Gloria.

Marie was good at doing things first. She had made a friend in their new neighborhood

right away—a girl as devoted to Giggletime Gloria as Marie herself. Meredith, who lived three houses up the hill and across Stony-brook Lane, had come with her mother to welcome the newcomers with a loaf of home-baked potato bread and a jar of apple butter. She had come, what's more, carrying her own brunette Giggletime Gloria.

Now Marie and Meredith spent most after-noons together. Their Glorias were best friends, too, only Meredith's Gloria had a Fab-ulous Filly to prance around on and pamper. The pink plastic horse had a long, luxurious mane and tail that could be combed, brushed, rolled, and permed.

Meredith had come up with the idea of using Cat as a Fabulous Filly for Marie's doll. The dog definitely looked curly after a secret session with the two girls and their rollers and bobby pins. The hair between his ears became shiny ringlets tied with a perky pink bow. Marie seemed to think Cat looked beautiful this way. Abbie thought the dog looked embarrassed.

Marie took the Yorkie up to Meredith's house for every visit now, despite the fact that the Fishers owned a mean, old black cat named Grandpa, who hissed and spit at every dog around.

Abbie didn't care enough to worry about Cat until he noticed something one day, when he had to walk his sister home.

As Abbie waited for Marie to get her doll stuff together, he saw that Grandpa wasn't hissing or spitting or doing any of his usual dog-hating tricks. The old cat, stretched out on the arm of a couch, was staring at Cat. Cat was rubbing his face with his paw, just like a cat. With his ears pricked up, he almost looked like a cat.

Then Grandpa leaped silently from his perch and rubbed up against Cat. The dog sat there patiently as old Grandpa butted his head against him, purring in a disgusting display of feline affection that made Abbie want to throw up. He decided right then and there never to have anything to do with Cat again.

He held to that decision for two days.

That was when he realized, with a nagging feeling of guilt, that his little sister had started calling Aunt Laura's dog Kitty-Cat.

MY DOG, CAT

"Come on, Kitty-Cat," she cooed. "Let's go get a big saucer of milk."

Abbie changed his mind that very instant.

Marie would ruin the dog if he let her. And it was a dog, after all, even if it wasn't the dog Abbie wanted. He was the big brother, and he wasn't going to let Marie get away with this. Abbie was going to start taking Cat along when he rode his bike. He could just take him on weekends, when no one from school was likely to see them together. The dog could easily fit in the basket between the handlebars. He'd pad it with an old towel. He'd teach the dog to like going fast. He'd teach it to catch the insects that buzzed by its face and swallow them.

He'd start tomorrow. He'd do it before Marie turned the Yorkie into some kind of misfit, instead of just a dog named Cat.

5. The Cat's Meow

The next morning, as Abbie walked past the open door of Marie's bedroom, he saw her putting a barrette in Cat's fur and sprinkling him with Apple Blossom cologne.

"Bug off," Abbie told his indignant little sister as he grabbed the dog from her arms, pushed past her, went into his own room, and locked the door.

"M-o-o-m!" Marie screamed down the hall. "Abbie took my dog!"

"It's not just your dog, honey." Abbie could hear his mother's voice drifting up the stairs. "Come help me in the kitchen, Marie. Let your brother have some time with the dog."

MY DOG, CAT

Abbie grinned with satisfaction as he heard his sister stomping down the hall. Her footsteps faded, but he could still hear her whining like an angry bee. It was almost worth being stuck with this runty little dog just to make Marie mad.

Abbie studied Cat's face. Or what he could see of it. The eyes and nose were buried by a cascade of silky black-and-brown hair, which Marie had been combing into a topknot every morning. Abbie carried the dog over to his desk, pushed aside his plastic ant farm and his chemistry set, and plunked Cat down. He opened the top drawer, took out his scissors, and studied the dog again, measuring the face like a movie director measuring a shot. Grabbing Cat's snout to steady his head, Abbie made a single, straight cut about half an inch above the barely visible dark brown eyes. A handful of fur fell away and revealed the dog's face completely. Abbie grinned. Now *this* looked like a dog.

Abbie snapped his fingers and Cat followed him down to the kitchen. His mother had promised to save the dry ice from the box of frozen crab Aunt Laura had brought them from

Baltimore. She knew how much he loved science stuff. Abbie opened the fridge and very carefully pulled out the plastic-wrapped block, dumping it in the green plastic basin from the sink. He carried the basin outside, where he could add water and watch the reaction.

Cat stayed beside him, even without a leash. It was Saturday. He could chance being outside with the Yorkie on a weekend. Nobody would see them together.

Abbie turned on the hose after he'd peeled away the plastic wrap, careful not to touch the frozen block of carbon dioxide. The dry ice looked like regular ice, only whiter. It was even better than the potato-powered clock he'd made for the science fair at his old school. As the water covered it, a thick white fog rose in the basin, spilling over the sides like a ghostly waterfall of mist.

Cat sniffed curiously at the spreading cloud, and Abbie fanned streamers of mist in the dog's direction.

Cat disappeared into the fog. The dog was no more than a shadowy ghost in the rolling whiteness.

The Cat's Meow

A voice came from behind Abbie, making him jump.

"You got dry ice there?"

Abbie turned to see Mike and Ryan, two boys from his class. They were both on bikes, and Ryan had a stack of red, green, and purple Frisbees in his bike basket.

"How'd you know?"

Abbie wished immediately he'd said something else—something smart or funny. But the boys popped their kickstands and came to kneel beside Abbie in the driveway, admiring the white cloud billowing from the bucket.

"You're Abbie, right?" Mike asked.

When Abbie only nodded, Mike continued, "Dry ice is so cool."

"Cold," Abbie corrected, smiling. Both visitors laughed.

Then Cat emerged from the whiteness, trailing wisps of vapor like a dog from another dimension. Abbie blushed. But Ryan whistled and tossed a Frisbee in Cat's direction, just over the little dog's head. Cat seemed to have springs on his feet as he leaped into the air and caught the small plastic disk in his jaws.

He dropped the Frisbee and barked once, sharply, as if to say, "This is my house and I'm in charge here." He trotted over to the visitors, stubby tail wagging.

"Your dog's got attitude," Ryan said admiringly. "All two ounces of him."

Abbie wasn't sure what to say.

"He's not, uh, he's not mine. He's my aunt's. We're just dog-sitting while she's on a trip."

"What's his name?" Ryan asked.

Abbie swallowed. "Catullus the Great." He said it fast, hoping it wouldn't sound as silly.

Mike laughed and stroked Cat's silky coat. "That's a major name for such a midget."

"I just call him Cat." Abbie could feel his cheeks flushing hotter as he said the name. But Ryan was throwing the disk again and Cat was catching it.

"He's as smooth as a cat, that's for sure," Ryan agreed.

A girl banged open the screen door on the house next door. She headed over to join them.

"Hey, guys." It was Heather, who was also in their class.

The Cat's Meow

"Hey, Abbie." Abbie was amazed. She'd never spoken to him, although he thought he'd seen her at the window, watching him.

"I like your dog." Heather bent to scratch between Cat's ears. "He's so adorable."

So that was it. It was Cat.

Abbie had known you could make fog by adding water to dry ice. He just hadn't known you could make friends by adding Cat.

6. To Bee or Not To Bee

"Wazzup?" Pete Street snatched the paper off Abbie's desk so fast, Abbie's grab for it netted only empty air.

Technically school was over for the day. But three fourth-grade classes had stayed after for the annual spelling bee, followed by a team photo of the spellers going to Districts.

Pete was peering at the paper, squinting at Abbie's handwriting as if he couldn't quite make it out.

"What's this supposed to be?" he challenged, thrusting the now crumpled paper under Abbie's nose. Jeff and Jason came up behind Pete and fanned out on either side of Abbie's desk.

"I was just fooling around," Abbie mumbled under his breath.

Jeff took the sheet Pete had dropped back on the desktop and began to read it out loud.

> *"Pete Street*
> *eats raw meat,*
> *knows how to cheat,*
> *has stinky feet,*
> *steals my seat."*

Jason began to titter, but one look from Pete stopped him.

Pete leaned down and put a hand on Abbie's shoulder, clutching a handful of his shirt.

"You better start talking, Runtface, before I stomp you all over with my 'stinky' feet."

Abbie bent away from Pete's menacing face hovering inches away from his nose. "I just like to make up words that rhyme," Abbie squeaked. "That's not a crime."

"Hey, that's a good one." Jeff guffawed, but a look from Pete silenced him.

"I don't give a flying fig about poetry. I want to know if you're dissing me?" Pete bellowed. Most of the kids in the crowded classroom, sitting on desks and lined up against the walls, waiting for the spelling bee to start, turned to see what was going on.

"No, Pete." Abbie blurted out a denial. "I wasn't dissing you. I wasn't even finished writing the poem yet."

"Oh yeah?" Pete smoothed out the paper and handed Abbie his pencil. "So finish."

Abbie scanned the words. Raw meat. Stinky feet.

"Pete Street is really neat," he said lamely, not even bothering to write the words down. Jeff and Jason were both laughing so hard now that no look from Pete could stop them.

Only now, Heather, Mike, and Ryan were there, too, standing behind Abbie's chair.

"I think it's a cute poem," Heather said, her hands on her hips.

"Give me that pencil," Pete growled. He turned the paper over and wrote "Abbott Williamson III."

"Okay, Mr. Poet. Here's a poem about *you.*"

The pencil in Pete's right hand was poised, but neither it nor Pete seemed to know what to write. Pete's left hand reached back and fiddled distractedly with the blue bandana stuffed, as always, in his back pocket.

"Abbott Williamson the Third looks like a bird," said Jeff, and sniggered.

"He knows lots of words," chimed in Heather.

"Just put that I'm a nerd," Abbie offered quietly, and Pete looked at him with surprise.

Pete wrote *nerd* in big letters and pushed the paper back under Abbie's nose. Then he crumpled it up and jammed it in his other back pocket.

The teacher entered the room and tapped a pointer on the blackboard, bringing instant silence.

"Today's spelling bee will use animal-related words. I know some of you will enjoy that." She smiled at Abbie.

"The first elimination round will begin with . . ." She began calling out names. Pete's name was in the first group. Pete looked uncomfortable, as if the neck of his T-shirt had suddenly gotten too tight and he couldn't breathe.

It was a dog that took Pete out. After spelling one word correctly, Pete was eliminated by "Doberman pinscher." He spelled it "Dobberman Pincher."

Abbie stopped thinking about Pete as the spelling bee went from round to round, with kids lining up to spell. Most of them left the room after missing a word and being called out. By the time Abbie made it to the final round, the room was almost cleared out.

Even Mike and Ryan had been eliminated.

It was down to two spellers: Abbie and Heather.

"Marsupial." Abbie spelled the word, sounding it out carefully in his head. Good thing they weren't required to define the words. Luckily, all they had to do was spell them.

Heather got hers right, too.

"The next word—" the teacher seemed to be pronouncing everything with extra care "—is basenji."

It was the first dog name since Doberman pinscher, and Abbie suddenly found himself thinking about Cat. He could definitely spell Yorkshire terrier, but it was a breed that didn't get much respect. Too often Yorkies were judged by their size.

MY DOG, CAT

Aunt Laura had said Yorkies were bred in the Middle Ages as hunting dogs because the English king wouldn't let peasants own full-size dogs for fear they'd poach the game in his deer parks. The king had actually sent men around with a piece of wood with a seven-inch circle cut out of it. He made it the law that any dog too big to fit through that circle would be taken away.

So the peasants in Yorkshire bred minia-ture terriers: feisty little dogs who would will-ingly tackle foxes or badgers twice as big as they were. And the thing was, the king never suspected they were hunting dogs. Being small saved them from the king's mean laws.

"Abbie?" the teacher's voice was sharp. "Are you still with us? The word is basenji." She paused, then added helpfully, "It's an African dog that doesn't really bark."

Cat barked all the time. Nothing got past Cat.

"Basenji," Abbie repeated, still thinking about the Yorkie. "B-a-s-s-e-n-j-i. Basenji."

"I'm sorry, Abbie, but that's not correct." The teacher turned. "Heather. The word is basenji."

"Basenji," Heather repeated. "B-a-s—" she raised her voice on the single *s* and continued—"e-n-j-i. Basenji."

"That is correct!" Polite applause erupted around the room. "Now I need my top ten spellers for the team photo. You'll all be going on to Districts."

An art teacher was adjusting his tripod as the winners lined up in two rows of five. He looked through his viewfinder and waggled a finger at Heather. "Young lady, I can't see the boy behind you at all."

Heather turned to Abbie. "I'm sorry," she whispered. "Here, you get in front of me. Shorter people are supposed to be in front."

Abbie grunted and changed places. Heather didn't know it, but he'd just composed an instant poem in his head:

Being small is not so bad,
For mice and bugs,
But it makes me mad.

7. Cat
in the Hat

The next morning when Abbie woke up, the sun streamed through his bedroom window. Cat, who had been sleeping on a pillow on the floor, jumped up and burrowed under the covers.

The dog tunneled under the blankets and up between Abbie's legs. He licked Abbie's toes and his kneecaps. He climbed on Abbie's body and licked his way up, past his belly button and his rib cage, to his neck and his chin.

"Hey, quit." Abbie laughed.

He reached for his glasses on the nightstand, slipping them on his nose. Cat licked Abbie's nose, smearing his glasses.

"I said quit," Abbie repeated, taking his glasses off and wiping them on the edge of his sheet. He jumped out of bed and began pulling out dresser drawers to find a sweatshirt, jeans, and his Baltimore Orioles baseball cap. It was Saturday. No school. No Pete Street.

Maybe the plan to meet Mike and Ryan at the public park for a round of Frisbee golf was a bad one. He'd promised to bring Cat along, but what if Pete showed up? Cat would be one more thing for him to sneer at.

Abbie drowned his Toastie Os in milk and watched Cat wrestling with a dirty sock, dragging it back and forth across the kitchen floor. Abbie almost didn't have to pick up his socks anymore. Cat kept them all corralled for him. His dad's handkerchiefs, too. Cat liked to keep all socks and handkerchiefs together.

"Hey, Mom," he called to her in the laundry room. "Can I take that old construction helmet Dad gave me?"

"It's yours now, Abbie. You don't have to ask," she called back, adding, "as long as you don't hit anybody with it. It is a hard hat, remember."

"Yeah, I know. I need it when I help the guys build a clubhouse," Abbie called back, slurping down the rest of the Toastie Os and putting the bowl on the floor for Cat to lick.

It was going to be a good day. He felt sure of it.

Pete was waiting at the park playground when Abbie pulled up. Mike was also there, looking worried. Ryan hadn't arrived yet.

"Hey, Runtface. Where are those cookies you promised me?" Abbie had completely forgotten his promise to bring Pete homemade chocolate chip cookies. But Pete was like an elephant—he never forgot. And he stomped those who did.

The bigger boy swaggered up to Abbie and Mike, both still on their bikes. Abbie flipped his baseball cap off his head and covered Cat, who sat next to the construction helmet in the bike basket.

"Your hat's moving." Pete had a mean smile, perfectly mimicked by Jeff and Jason, who stood behind him. Mike sat on his bike beside Abbie, staring at Pete without blinking. No one else was in sight.

"Leave us alone, Pete." Mike's voice was low and expressionless. "We're not bothering you."

"Yes. You are." Pete snatched at the cap covering Cat. "Well, lookie here. It's Runtface Two. Your dog looks just like you."

Jeff and Jason made hearty noises of agreement. Pete scooped Cat out of the basket before Abbie knew what was happening. He tossed the little dog to the ground, where Cat landed lightly on all fours, true to his namesake. Pete nudged the dog roughly with his sneaker. "No wonder you tried to hide this rat. If Tiny was here, she'd swallow him in one gulp."

Pete laughed as if he'd made the best joke ever. Jeff and Jason laughed along with him. Abbie didn't laugh, and neither did Mike.

"What's the matter with you guys? It's just a *little* joke." Pete started laughing all over again as he reached for Cat. But the dog dodged effortlessly out of his reach. Pete lunged, and Cat took off around the swings and the jungle gym with Pete and his henchmen giving chase.

"Pete's stupider than he looks if he thinks he can outrun a dog," Mike whispered to

Abbie. "But let's get out of here before he figures out that a little dog is way faster than a big ox."

"This way, Cat," Abbie shouted as he and Mike took off in a spray of gravel, riding for the far side of the fenced playground. "Come on, boy."

Cat turned and breezed past Pete's reaching hands, dashing through a tiny dip under the chain-link around the play area.

"Come back here, you!" Pete screamed, jabbing a finger in Abbie's direction. "I'll stomp all over you and your little dog, too."

"He must think we're Munchkins and he's the Wizard of Oz," Mike shouted to Abbie as they pedaled furiously away.

"He's not the Wizard. He's the Wicked Witch," Abbie yelled back.

Abbie kept pedaling without turning around or even taking time to push up his glasses from where the sweat had made them slip.

They screeched to a halt a block from the park and Abbie bent down to scoop a panting Cat back into his basket. Cat licked his

fingers and his sweaty palms, wagging a joy-
ous greeting. Ryan pedaled up at that moment, on his way to the park.

"What's up?" he asked.

"You missed it," Mike answered, reaching
over to scratch between the Yorkie's silky ears.
"Seems like, for a little dog, Cat's bigger than
he looks."

8. Rat-a-tat Cat

"It's definitely war." Ryan was obviously excited by the prospect. "You have to help us finish our fort, Abbie, so we'll be ready."

They'd ditched their bikes at the bottom of the hill behind Ryan's house. Cat ran ahead of them on his leash as they threaded their way between sassafras trees and rhododendron bushes. Abbie carried his yellow construction helmet up the hill in one hand and Cat's lead in the other.

As they broke out of the woods into a small clearing, Abbie could see FORT RY-MI clearly marked with a hand-painted sign, the white paint running into stringy tails on every letter except *f.* The sign was propped against two large, wooden packing crates on the edge of the clearing. Nearby was a blue plastic tarp, tied with clothesline rope between three small maples. One flap of the tarp hung down, forming a sort of back door. A cardboard sign pinned to the door read KEEP OUT.

"This is it," Mike announced proudly, pulling back the flap to reveal a dark interior with orange plastic, milk-crate stools. An inflatable swim raft that needed more air was propped against a side wall. Mike entered and switched on a flashlight that was taped to the roof of one crate with duct tape. Its weak beam made the place look spooky, but the cheese-and-peanut-butter crackers Ryan pulled out of his backpack made it seem homey immediately.

"What do you think?" Mike asked after giving Abbie a minute to look around. Abbie studied the eyeholes cut in the crate walls facing the clearing and the old ice chest filled with X-Men comic books.

"Awesome," Abbie said, spitting crumbs. He unhooked Cat's leash so the dog could explore, too.

"We can change the name as soon as we get more paint," Mike offered. Cat nibbled cracker crumbs off the tops of Mike's sneakers.

"Yeah," Ryan agreed. "How does 'Fort Ry-Mi-Ab' sound?"

"Or 'Fort Mi-Ry-Ab'?" Mike suggested.

"How about 'Ab-Mi-Ry'?" Abbie winked at his friends as he asked the question. It was an honor for the new guy to have the first two letters of his name included at all.

Ryan and Mike laughed agreeably.

"This looks pretty finished to me," Abbie added. "What else do we need to do to it?"

"Add a second floor," confided Ryan, and Abbie glanced at the tarp above him. "We're going to build a platform as soon as we get some wood. Then we can post lookouts so we'll know who's coming."

Cat's ears went up and his head swiveled toward the clearing.

"Good idea." Abbie stuffed another cracker in his mouth and almost choked on it when a voice boomed: "Hey, creep-os. You can't hide from Pete Street."

Rat-a-tat Cat

War whoops from Jason and Jeff made the hair stand up on the nape of Abbie's neck. Mike stood and switched off the flashlight. Ryan peered through a set of eyeholes and gasped. Cat began to bark, bouncing around like a windup toy in the leaf mold and tree roots of the fort's floor.

"Watch out!" Ryan yelled, ducking as a water balloon splattered through the eyeholes on the fort's front wall, spraying Ryan's jeans. "They came armed," he cried. "They've got a whole laundry basket full of water balloons. What are we gonna do?"

Ryan had been yelling the words over Cat's barking, but the dog stopped suddenly. There was an endless moment of silence when Mike ventured a quick glance out another set of eyeholes.

"Duck!" Mike shouted as two more water balloons splatted noisily against the fort.

"Rats," Ryan muttered. "If we'd had a look-out, this wouldn't have happened."

"Too late for that now." Abbie crept to an eyehole for a quick look, just barely dodging away without getting an eyeful of water. Water was starting to drip on them through the frayed spots in the tarp.

"We could blind them with my flashlight," Mike suggested hopefully.

"In broad daylight?" Abbie asked.

"How about bombarding them with rolled-up comic books?" Ryan opened the ice chest and looked at their stash. "I just wish we had a rocket launcher or a Gatling gun." He raised an arm, the finger pointing, and began making "rat-a-tat-tat" noises.

"We're not throwing X-Men," Mike objected. "You can launch the Spider-mans, but we only have three of those. Besides, whoever steps outside to throw will get drenched."

"Pete really has us pinned down," Ryan agreed ruefully. "There's no way to escape."

"Hey! Where's Cat?" Abbie searched for the dog. But the corners of the fort were empty. Cat wasn't under the tarp flap, either.

"Think he ran away?" Mike asked.

"If he deserted under attack, he can't be a member of the club," Ryan stated. "Even a dog has to be brave to be part of Fort Ry-Mi-Ab."

Abbie nodded sadly. He guessed all the whooping and splatting had scared the little Yorkie. It sounded like missiles were raining down on them. Jeff and Jason were hee-hawing like mules. Abbie felt a little scared himself, though he'd never admit it to Ryan or Mike. He really couldn't blame Cat for running away.

Defeat loomed over them like the blackest thunder cloud. "Pete's gonna take our fort," Ryan whispered. Mike blinked at him as if he couldn't quite grasp the words.

"Come out of there, you creep-os. Come out on your hands and knees and we'll only get you a *little* wet." Pete sounded as if he was enjoying himself immensely.

"*Crawl* out?" Abbie shook his head, his mouth set in a grim line. "I'm not crawling for Pete Street. I'm not crawling for anybody."

"You think maybe the cavalry will come riding to the rescue, like in a Western?" Mike snorted. "I don't think so."

"Cat!" Abbie looked at the ball of fur jumping into his lap. "Where'd you go?" The dog happily licked Abbie's chin and cheek, letting something blue fall out of his mouth.

Ryan caught the knotted blue cloth before it hit the ground. He held it up, staring at it in speechless wonder.

"Is that what I think it is?" Mike breathed. "Is it Pete Street's precious bandana?"

"Unbelievable." Ryan whispered the word. "Your dog just delivered our salvation."

Abbie wondered if Ryan was cracking under the strain of Pete's attack. Cat was a mess, his tan face splattered with mud.

"It's a stupid bandana. How is that going to help us?"

"Don't you see?" Mike was pacing in a tight circle. Cat jumped down to follow him. Apparently the dog thought it was some kind of new game: walk as fast as you can without going anywhere. "I don't know how he got this out of Pete's pocket, but Pete Street never goes anywhere without it. He keeps his valuables tied up in it."

"Then he's going to kill us even worse than he was before," Abbie protested.

"No, he won't. Not if he ever wants to see

his stuff again." Ryan held the mud-stained bandana above his head in triumph. "This bandana is our hostage."

Mike put his lips to the nearest eyehole opening and shouted: "Hey, Pete. Checked your bandana lately?"

A well-aimed water balloon nailed Mike, and he backed up sputtering. "Dump it out," he ordered, turning to Ryan. "Let's see what Pete Street considers valuable."

There were sounds of shouting and running feet outside.

Some coins and a folded piece of paper fell out when Ryan untied the first knot. There was more, but Cat seized the end and started wrestling Ryan for it, clearly loving this unexpected tug-of-war.

Mike unfolded the paper and a photo fell out. "It's Heather's school picture and that Pete Street–stinky feet poem you wrote, Abbie. I'm telling you, this guy is losing it. Why would he carry this stuff around?"

"Because he likes Heather, and it made him feel important that somebody wrote a poem about him," Ryan offered, lifting Cat right off the ground without succeeding in shaking him off.

"Who carries stuff in a bandana anyway?" Mike scoffed. "Hasn't he ever heard of a wallet?"

"There are a lot of things Pete Street has never heard of," Ryan said, trying to fool Cat by letting go and then grabbing the bandana and jerking it hard. But Cat still hung on. "Like fairness and sportsmanship and—"

"Hey, creep-os . . ." Pete's voice was shouting at them. He stopped and backtracked, using an almost peacemaking tone. "You in the fort. Do you have my stuff?"

Ryan finally wrenched the bandana, now torn, away from Cat. He wiggled a piece of it through one of the eyeholes. "Do you see it, Pete?" Ryan yelled. "It's your bandana."

There was complete silence for what seemed like a full minute. "I don't believe it!" Pete's voice boomed with anger. "I hid that in a place where it wouldn't get messed up with water balloons. Jammed it under a tree root." They heard rustling as Pete bent down on his knees to search. "I don't know how *you* got it, but—" Abbie heard the sound of Jason sniggering, and then a thump.

"You didn't have to push me," Jason whined.

"But," Pete continued, "if you give it back without looking at my stuff, we'll go away and call this a draw. No hard feelings," Pete sounded as if he was trying to be sincere. "No ambushes."

"Yeah, like we'd believe you," Mike muttered, but not quite loud enough that Pete could hear him.

Cat grabbed the bandana back from Ryan and trotted over to Abbie with it.

Abbie picked the coins out of the leaf mold and shoved them, along with the refolded poem and the photo, back on top of the other stuff in the bandana. Then he retied it without looking at Ryan or Mike.

"Okay!" he shouted. "You send Jeff and Jason back down the hill *with* the rest of your water balloons and we'll hand over the bandana." He paused and looked at Mike and Ryan. "Without looking. I promise."

Ryan had his eyes glued to a peephole, and he waved his hand wildly. "They're doing it!

They're really doing it. Jeff and Jason are leaving."

Abbie got up and brushed the bandana off as best he could. He lifted the tarp flap and walked solemnly out of the clubhouse and around to where Pete was standing, extending a hand with the bandana dangling from it. Cat followed, sticking close to his heels.

"That dog," growled Pete, taking one look at Cat's muddy face. "That dog stole it." He grabbed the bandana and shoved it in his jeans pocket. "Nothing else could get in a hole that small." He took a step toward Abbie, his hands clenched in fists.

"You said no hard feelings," Abbie reminded him. "No ambushes."

Pete stopped, but his hands remained clenched. "Maybe not today, Runtface." Pete's held-in anger felt like a cold water balloon breaking down Abbie's neck. "But you'll pay. You and that mudball." He turned on his heel and walked rapidly out of the clearing and out of sight.

Mike and Ryan emerged from the shadow of the fort to stand beside Abbie, watching

Pete go. Ryan carried Abbie's construction helmet. Mike held a water balloon in either hand.

"We found these behind the fort," Mike explained, kneeling down and breaking first one and then the other balloon into the hard hat, like eggs into a mixing bowl. "They missed the fort and landed on leaf mold, so they didn't break."

"And you're putting water in my helmet because . . . ?" Abbie's voice was incredulous.

"Because Cat needs a bath," Ryan finished. "That's one thing Pete Street was actually right about."

Laughing and splashing, the three friends sloshed Cat into the hat and rinsed all the mud out of his fur.

"So we're going to change the name tomorrow," Ryan told Abbie. "I remembered where we can get some paint."

"The name of the fort? Did you decide on 'Ry-Mi-Ab' or 'Mi-Ry-Ab'?" asked Abbie, grinning at the other two survivors of the Battle of Pete Street.

"Neither," Mike answered. "We're going to

call it 'Ry-Mi-Ab-Ca.' We have to include *all* the members."

Abbie looked down at Cat's dripping face and nodded. "You can't tell by looking at him," Abbie said, "but Cat's our secret weapon."

9. Cat/Burglar

Abbie sat at the kitchen counter and stamped a tulip cookie cutter in the thick white dough rolled out on the floured countertop. He was helping his mother and Marie cut sugar cookies in the shapes of birds and flowers. It had been two months since they moved here. Half of that time being tortured by Pete Street—the first half. But since that day at the fort, Abbie had anxiously avoided one-on-one run-ins with the bully. There had been close calls, though. One time when Abbie was late for class, he'd seen Pete walking down the empty hallway toward him. But Abbie quickly ducked into the science lab and asked Mr. Brell a question about microscopes.

Besides, Abbie had other things to worry about now, too. Tomorrow was the last day of school. Next week Aunt Laura would get back from her trip, and Cat would leave.

Abbie couldn't let himself think about that.

As they worked at the counter, Abbie watched the dog jump up on a chair, using it as a stepping stone to jump onto the kitchen table. Cat seemed to be playing follow-the-leader with his mother's gray tabby, settling in a square patch of sunlight beside the tabby, stretching when she stretched, totally comfortable being a dog called Cat. Abbie had made up a poem about it. It went:

> *Cat can get in anywhere,*
> *All he is is nose and hair.*
> *As a dog he's not too lame,*
> *Doesn't mind his crazy name.*

Abbie popped a grape into his mouth with flour-covered fingers. He was experimenting with different kinds of food to see if there was something that would make him grow faster. He hadn't tried spinach yet. It worked for Popeye, making the squinting sailor super strong, but spinach? Yuck! Abbie couldn't see why growth food had to taste bad.

So far, he'd tried jelly beans, bananas, and marmalade toast. He tossed a grape to Cat, who caught it neatly and dropped it on the table, nosing it around and licking it all over before gulping it down.

Abbie sighed and pushed the remaining grapes aside. That was the test, of course. If Cat ate it, it couldn't be growth food. And, so far, Cat had eaten everything.

"I'm sure Aunt Laura will let you visit whenever you like," said his mom thoughtfully, watching him watch the dog. She was rolling out more cookie dough on the countertop.

Then she put the rolling pin down with a clunk and dusted the flour off her hands. "I've made up my mind," she announced without waiting for comment. "As soon as these cookies are out of the oven, the four of us—you, me, Marie, and Cat—are going to town."

The trouble with having short legs is, you have to take two steps for everyone else's one.

Abbie had that problem sometimes when he walked with Ryan.

Now Cat was having the same trouble with Abbie's mom. She rushed from the drug store to the shoe store to the stationery store, in a hurry to run her errands. People hardly had time to avoid stepping on the Yorkie, let alone stop and admire him. The only chance was while Abbie waited outside the stores with Cat, but each time, before he knew it, his mother was out and hurrying to the next place. Even Marie was out of breath.

"Mom." Abbie caught hold of his mother's purse strap. "Mom, you're moving too fast. We're going to have to carry Cat."

"Yeah, Mommy," complained Marie. "Carry me, too."

Abbie's mother sighed and looked at the watch on her wrist. "Can you piggyback Marie for a while?" she asked Abbie, reaching down to pick up Cat and slide him into her roomy purse. The flap rested loosely on Cat's head. He looked like a fox peering out of his den.

Abbie hoisted Marie onto his back, making loud choking noises as his sister wrapped her

arms around his neck. "Leave me enough room to breathe, okay?"

"Giddyup, giddyup!" Marie bounced up and down on her brother's back, excited to get a ride. Sticky LifeSaver slobber trickled down her chin and landed on the back of Abbie's neck.

"Ease up, will you?" Abbie had a wiry strength that his dad kept promising would translate into a growth spurt, but Marie was testing his limits with her bouncing. He was wiping at the back of his neck when he heard his mother cry out.

"Stop! Come back! Stop! Thief!"

A young man in khakis and a leather jacket was quickly disappearing into the crowd of shoppers. He had Abbie's mother's purse dangling from one hand. A shrill barking erupted from the purse as the man dodged into the throng of people and vanished from sight.

Abbie almost dropped Marie on the pavement as he started to gallop after the thief, but his sister held on tight.

"Wait, Abbie, wait," his mom called, reaching out a shaking hand to stop him. "I don't want you getting hurt."

She was lifting Marie off his back, shaking her head in bewilderment. "I've never been robbed before. Not even in the city. Can you believe it? That guy has my driver's license and all my credit cards. I had almost one hundred dollars cash in that bag. All gone. Stolen by a purse snatcher!"

"That guy stole Cat, too, Mom!" Abbie reminded her, pulling out of her grasp and following the sound of the Yorkie's barking. "I have to get him back." Security guards in brown uniforms came running out of the big Penney's store, clutching walkie-talkies. His mother gestured after Abbie.

"That's my son, officers. He's chasing the purse snatcher who got all my money. He got my sister's little Yorkshire terrier, too. In my purse. You can hear him barking. . . ."

But the guards had already taken off, threading their way along the crowded sidewalks. There were two of them. One followed Abbie. The other circled around, disappearing down an alley, as if he knew a shortcut.

MY DOG, CAT

It wasn't hard to track the fleeing thief. In fact, Abbie found it difficult to believe the guy didn't have enough sense to ditch the purse, or at least dump the frantically barking Yorkie. The sound penetrated the hum of other shoppers' voices and drowned out the soothing music playing over the Town Center's outdoor speakers.

It was like following a blip on a radar screen. Each way the thief turned, Cat's barking kept up its steady, ear-piercing volume. The wide sidewalks cleared as people made way, alerted by the insistent yelping, until the two guards converged on the purse snatcher. The thief stood with his hands halfway up, an almost comical expression of exasperation on his face. A brown leather purse dangled from one shoulder, swaying with a life of its own as a small black nose poked its way out from beneath the flap.

The thief had two other purses over the same shoulder, their straps entangled so that he couldn't have dumped one without dumping them all. He let all three slide down his arm in an obvious gesture of surrender.

Abbie reached for his mom's purse, shaking the strap loose. He drew the excited Yorkie out of it, putting the handbag on his own shoulder while he cuddled Cat in his arms. The barking stopped so quickly, it sounded as though someone had flipped a switch. Cat was all relieved licks and tiny whines of happiness now that he was in Abbie's arms.

The Yorkie smeared its tongue so enthusiastically over his glasses, it was impossible to see. Abbie was rubbing them off, as best he could, on Cat's fur when his mother and Marie caught up with them. "Oh, you wonderful heroes," gushed his mom, gathering both boy and dog into her arms. "You really saved the day."

"It was all Cat, not me," argued Abbie, pushing out of his mother's arms.

His mother took his glasses and cleaned them with her shirt. "I'm so proud of you both," she said.

"And well you should be, ma'am," said a guard with an open notebook, coming up to them and scratching Cat between his high, pricked ears. "I don't believe I've ever seen a more effective mugging deterrent than that little pup. I guess this is what they mean when they say good things come in small packages."

Abbie had heard those very same words so many times. He'd never believed them, not for a minute. The funny thing was, he believed them now.

"Our public relations lady is going to want a photo of your little canine hero for the *Wakefield Shopping News,* and I have a few questions, if you don't mind," continued one of the security guards. The other had taken charge of the slump-shouldered purse snatcher, who was hemmed in by the gawking crowd.

Abbie put Cat down on the green carpeted entrance to the department store. Several people in the crowd applauded. Abbie wondered later if the clapping startled Cat. Or maybe the green fooled him into thinking he was on grass. Or maybe the excitement was just too much for a bladder that had to be the size of a pea.

Cat/Burglar

Whatever the reason, Cat lifted his back leg and relieved himself in a tiny yellow stream against the shiny black shoe of the thief.

10. Cat-Astrophe

Abbie couldn't help it. He still sometimes wished he'd wake up one morning, look over at Cat, and discover the Yorkie had turned into a Great Dane overnight. Or at least a German shepherd.

Cat was a wonderful dog. There was no question about it. The Yorkie's photo had been in the *Wakefield Shopping News*. His mom had even grilled the dog his very own T-bone steak after their run-in with the purse snatcher. That had been a week ago.

Abbie looked down at Cat, walking confidently beside him. His dad had promised they'd get a new dog after Aunt Laura came to

pick up Cat tonight. They'd get the big power-
ful "Killer" dog Abbie had always wanted.

He kicked at a pile of gravel in the gutter,
leftover from last winter's snow plowing. It
made a satisfying skittering sound as it fanned
out across the road.

Abbie was on his way to the post office to
mail some letters and a small package for his
mother. With his bike in the shop for its summer tune-up, he was walking the half mile
into Wakefield.

Cat trotted cheerfully at his side, ears
pricked forward, nose to the ground, taking
in all the smells and messages other animals had left behind. The little terrier
seemed to bounce when he walked, broadcast-
ing a happy confidence that Abbie envied.
The thin, red leather leash dangled loosely
between boy and dog. Cat stuck close to
Abbie's feet, leash or no leash.

The post office was a small brick building
with an American flag flying out front. It was
just a block downhill from where their road
crossed Main Street. Across from the post office
was Arnie's, the favorite summer hangout of

just about every kid in town. Even from a block away, Abbie could see that the place was crowded. Cars jammed the parking lot and kids crammed around all the outdoor tables.

Abbie waved to Mike and Ryan, and they waved back. He felt in the pockets of his shorts. Did he have enough change rattling around in there for a milkshake?

No. He had a dime, two pennies, and a small wad of lint. Abbie resigned himself to doing his mother's errand and heading right back home. Maybe she'd pay him for his help. Then he could come back and get a shake with his friends.

"Hey, Runtface. Did you know you have a rat following you?"

Pete materialized from around the corner of the post office as if he'd been lying in wait. His dog, Tiny, stalked menacingly beside him.

Pete grabbed the letters and package out of Abbie's hand and waved them high overhead.

"Writing away for growth hormones?" Pete mocked.

"Give those back." Abbie stretched a hand out for the package but couldn't get close to it.

Cat barked reprovingly at Pete and stood stiff-legged, facing the big Akita. Tiny growled and curled back a black lip to show a flash of white.

Pete leaned in a leisurely way against a telephone pole. His two lieutenants, Jeff and Jason, had come up on either side of him, mimicking Pete's assured posture and the smirk on the taller boy's face.

"I said, do you know there's a rat following you? You really picked the right dog, didn't you? A runt for a runt." Pete laughed. Jeff and Jason took their cue from Pete. They laughed, too.

Tiny was still growling, a deep rumbling sound. Tiny wasn't on a leash, but Pete had one hand on the dog's thick leather collar. The other still held Abbie's letters and package over his head.

Now Pete removed the collar hand and pointed a finger at Abbie. Tiny took a step forward, snarling with a menacing intensity that revealed teeth the size of steak knives. Abbie felt like he had a ball of cold spaghetti in his stomach. He wanted to run. He wanted to hide. But he couldn't. Not while everybody was watching.

And it felt as if everyone in the whole world, including everyone from the fourth grade at Wakefield Elementary, was sitting across from the post office. Watching him. Wondering what he'd do next.

Abbie wondered himself.

II. Cat —
Not Gnat

Abbie couldn't take his eyes off Tiny's menacing approach. The dog's black eyes, with their glint of yellow, held Abbie's eyes so that he couldn't move.

All sounds of laughter, all voices across the street, even the traffic seemed to stop. All Abbie could hear was the beating of his heart thumping so loudly inside his chest, he wondered if Cat could hear it too.

He stepped back in an involuntary movement that he felt sure smacked of cowardice. He wouldn't have any friends left after this. Pete might as well finish him off, here and now. It would be better than this hot, burning humiliation.

Cat—Not Gnat

Abbie glanced down, expecting to see Cat crowding between his feet. But Cat was out in front of him, straining at the leash, like a tiny barrier between Abbie and disaster.

The dog was trembling.

But not in fear. Cat was trembling in anger. His fur was so puffed up, he looked twice his usual size. Cat growled, making a sound that was both deep and doglike. Abbie was surprised a Yorkie could make a sound like that.

Tiny kept growling, but she glanced over her shoulder at Pete.

At that very moment, Cat lunged forward, a stuffed toy gone berserk. The leash was torn from Abbie's numb fingers as Cat charged Tiny's huge paws. It wrapped around Tiny's front legs, then unwound as Cat circled one way and then the other.

The startled Akita snapped at the creature circling her feet. She missed completely, but Abbie could hear the click of teeth. He suddenly remembered Pete bragging about how Akitas were Japanese fighting dogs used in the ring to kill bears.

Cat was grabbing mouthfuls of fur from Tiny's back legs now, worrying the top hairs,

pulling out small globs of thick brown under-coat.

Tiny took a step backward, confused by this unexpected turn of events. She whined, turning again to her master. Pete's lips were pressed tightly together. To Abbie, everything seemed to be moving in slow motion as Pete drew back his arm and threw the letters and package at Cat. The letters floated harmlessly to the pavement. The package sailed in Cat's direction like a bomb.

But Cat was too quick. He dodged with the ease and grace of a matador playing with a maddened bull. Pete missed completely. The package hit the ground with a thud as Cat returned to the business of harrying Tiny with nips and barks and lunges.

The Yorkie managed to jump high enough to catch the thick fur of Tiny's chest hair and hang there, dangling in midair, as the distracted Akita twisted in a half circle, trying to keep an eye on her angry master and her attacker at the same time.

Suddenly, Abbie heard an explosion of voices. He glanced in the direction of Arnie's and was surprised to see people lined along the curb, watching and pointing. Not at him. They were pointing at his dog, the tiny, tenacious terrier with no fear of giants.

The Akita shook herself, the way a dog shakes when a bothersome flea is caught in its coat. Cat flew from side to side like a trapeze artist on a circus swing. Another hard shake bounced Cat onto the pavement, where he rolled twice before regaining his footing.

People in the watching crowd began to boo. "Hey, you big bully, get out of here," called a girl's voice. "Go pick on somebody your own size."

Abbie wasn't sure whether the girl was talking to Pete or Pete's dog. There were catcalls and more boos as Tiny moved forward to tower over Cat, the fearsome hulk of the Akita dwarfing the small warrior at her feet. Abbie looked at Pete to see if he would call off his dog.

Pete's ears had turned red and his mouth was set in a grim line. "Get that rat," Pete called, his voice surprisingly shrill. "It's not a rat, even. It's a gnat. Get it, Tiny!"

Tiny lurched forward, black lips curled back, teeth showing. Cat retreated, barking angrily. The little Yorkie squeezed underneath the closest car, a low-slung red sportscar parked in front of the post office. The leash trailed behind him like a dragon's tail. From under the automobile, Cat sent out a string of noisy challenges. Abbie wondered if it was Cat's way of saying, "Nah, nah-nah, nah, nah. You can't get me."

Tiny stepped off the curb, dropped to her chest, and rammed her big furry body halfway under the car, teeth snapping. Gravel pinged against the curb and the bottom of the car.

Abbie was afraid. He'd been digging his fingernails into the palms of his hands so hard he'd left marks. But now his hands balled into fists. For the first time, he wasn't afraid for himself. He was afraid for Cat.

As Tiny backed up to try another angle of attack, Abbie took one step forward and shouted sharply, "No, Tiny! Bad dog!" The stern sound of command in his voice surprised even Abbie.

"No!" he repeated. Tiny stared at him in complete bewilderment. Then the dog's bushy tail swung down and fastened itself between her legs.

Tiny shuffled backward, trying to get behind Pete, but Pete sidestepped, hissing, "Stupid dog." He reached down and swatted her halfheartedly on her furry rump. It couldn't have hurt, but Tiny yelped anyway, her black eyes puzzled. Pete's whole face was a splotchy red now.

Pete turned on his heel, snapping his fingers at Tiny. Or maybe he was snapping them at Jeff and Jason, because all three followed him. Abbie could hear Pete saying, "Let's get out of this stupid place." Whatever else Pete had to say was lost in the burst of applause from across the street.

"Hey, Abbie!" yelled Ryan, waving his long arm in a triumphant salute. "Come on over and bring Superdog there with you."

Abbie bent and picked up the package and the letters from where they lay on the sidewalk. He brushed them off and placed them in the big blue metal mailbox outside the post office's double glass doors.

"Come on over, Abbie. It's my treat," called Heather. "Do you want a shake?"

Abbie scooped up the dog that now sat on his foot. He could hear cars moving again. He

could hear kids laughing and joking. Abbie
closed his eyes for a moment, trying to sort it
all out. Pete hadn't punched him. Tiny hadn't
eaten Cat. Both of them had been big enough
to stand up for themselves. Or, more to the
point, to stand up for each other.

Abbie joined his friends on the cement
bench around one of the round cement tables
with its broad green-and-white umbrella. "A
vanilla shake would be great. Thanks," Abbie
told Heather. "It's Cat's favorite."

Heather reached out to ruffle the silky fur
on the little dog's head. "I can't believe you did
that. I would have been so scared," she said,
scratching between Cat's ears. "I guess my
mom is right when she says it's not the size of
the dog in your heart, it's the size of the heart
in your dog."

A boy at the next table slapped Abbie on
the back and reached across Heather to pet
Cat. "That's some dog. He's as good as any
watchdog."

Abbie put Cat on the tabletop and let the
Yorkie slurp big gulps from the milkshake
cup.

"Cat's a good name for him. He drinks

milkshakes just like a cat," Heather said, and giggled.

"Cat is *all* dog," Abbie replied, grinning at the sight of milkshake foam dripping from the terrier's whiskers. He could feel Cat's eyes on his face and his throat suddenly tightened, making it hard to swallow. He couldn't meet Cat's eyes. Instead, he looked at his own black sneakers. He felt funny.

Maybe it was a headache from drinking the cold milkshake too fast. Maybe it was that growth spurt his parents kept talking about. Or maybe it was the edge of fear slicing through his brain. Fear that Cat was the only dog he'd ever feel this way about. The only dog he'd ever love quite like this.

And by tomorrow, Cat would be gone.

12. If I Had Three Wishes

"So what kind of dog do you think you want?" Abbie's dad was looking through the classified section of the newspaper. The page was open to the column headed "Pets."

What kind of dog did he want? It was a straightforward enough question. But Abbie heard the words his father hadn't said, the missing end of that deceptively simple question: What kind of a dog do you want *instead of Cat*?

Before Abbie could say anything, a horn honked in the driveway. "It's Aunt Laura!" squealed Marie, dancing with her Giggletime Gloria doll around the living room. "Aunt Laura said she'd bring me something!"

Aunt Laura was tanned and smiling, baby Lee bouncing on her hip, almost like last time. Uncle Jerry had come along, too, but he was still getting stuff out of the car. Marie's long-haired calico cat rubbed a warm welcome against Aunt Laura's ankles.

"Laura! You look wonderful! Your trip obviously agreed with you!" Abbie's mom clasped her sister in a warm embrace that enfolded both mother and baby.

"It was terrific, Shar! Mother and Dad Stevens were great, and Jerry said he'd get me any souvenirs my heart desired. You should see the stuff packed in the back of the car. And we brought this back for you, Marie." Aunt Laura handed Abbie's wide-eyed little sister a package wrapped in silver paper with a big pink bow.

When Marie tore the box open, she found a brand-new purple Fabulous Filly with a luxurious long golden mane and tail.

"Oh boy, oh boy. I thought Cat made a good Filly, but not as good as this one," she said. Cat's tail thumped at the mention of his name. "What did you bring Abbie? Huh, Aunt Laura, huh? Do Abbie next."

"Marie." Their mother's voice carried an unspoken warning against sounding greedy.

"I don't want anything," protested Abbie, clutching Cat to his chest so tightly that the dog turned and began thoroughly licking his chin. Abbie pushed his glasses back up on his sweaty nose. It was a lie, of course. He wanted Cat. He wanted the little dog with the funny name more than he had ever wanted anything in his entire life.

"And how is little sweet pea doing?" cooed Aunt Laura, scratching Cat under the chin and talking in that cute voice some people use for babies and small animals. "You ready to go home, Cat? Wait till you—"

Marie grabbed their aunt's hand and dragged her into the corner to admire her Giggletime Gloria dollhouse.

Abbie felt dizzy. The living room with its familiar objects—the TV, the fireplace, the maple hutch lined with his mom's porcelain cat figurines—seemed to spin around him. He closed his eyes and tried to take a deep breath, but his chest felt tight.

When he opened his eyes, his dad's big yellow tom was staring down at him mockingly

from his perch atop the hutch. The cat's tail twitched. It was one place that was too high for a dog to jump, even a dog named Cat. The tom's green gaze regarded Abbie without sympathy, as if to say, "Well, what did you expect? This is a cat family."

This was it then. This was the moment when Aunt Laura would take Cat from his arms. Abbie knew all too well what being short felt like, but this was the first time he'd ever felt small. It felt like his heart was shrinking inside him.

His mom took baby Lee out of Aunt Laura's arms. His pretty young aunt, her blond ponytail bobbing, placed one hand on each of Abbie's shoulders and looked him square in the eyes.

"Abbie, it was a wonderful trip, like I already said. Wait until you—"

Uncle Jerry banged through the front screen door just at that moment, interrupting her. He was staggering under the weight of a fold-up playpen, a diaper bag, and a brown, leather cat carrier.

Abbie knew immediately what the carrier was for. Cat would go into that carrier to leave.

Cat, who caught flies in midair and wasn't afraid of bullies, would be crammed into that silly cat carrier. It wasn't fair.

Abbie tried to say something but couldn't get any words past the lump in his throat. His mouth opened and closed silently. He felt like he couldn't breathe. He took off his glasses and wiped them on the hem of his shirt, even though Cat hadn't licked them. They seemed blurred.

His heart was pounding so loudly in his ears that, at first, Abbie wasn't sure he'd heard Aunt Laura right when she said: "Wait until you see what your Uncle Jerry got me in California. You'll get a kick out of this, Abbie, since you like dogs so much. This is the kind of dog we saw movie stars walking on the beach. I tell you, I fell in love with this little beauty at first sight. It's so unusual. I think it looks more like some kind of exotic bird than a dog."

She turned as she spoke to fumble with the latch of the cat cage. From the dark interior of the box, she withdrew the strangest animal Abbie had ever seen outside of a zoo. It might be a dog, but it looked like some kind of weird rooster. It was hairless, a patchy tan-and-white color. A flowing mane of silky white hair fell over and around its large, thin, feathered ears. It started yipping as soon as it caught sight of Cat. The dog had a shrill bark, as tiny and pointed as its fragile body. A sparse tan-and-white beard looked strangely out of place hanging from its delicate muzzle.

"This is Byrd," gushed Aunt Laura, holding the creature high so everyone could see. Abbie heard his mother gasp. "He's a Chinese crested," Aunt Laura continued. "That's a variation of the Mexican hairless. He weighs only five pounds, and I think he looks like some kind of plumed jungle fowl. I decided to name him after Sir William Byrd, the famous fifteenth-century English composer. Isn't that just perfect? A dog named Byrd." Aunt Laura giggled at her own joke.

"So now we're a two dog family. Two dogs with the weirdest names on the block." Uncle Jerry sounded resigned. "And that reminds me of our surprise for you, Ab."

Aunt Laura broke in, too excited to let Uncle Jerry reveal the surprise. "We're getting you a dog, Abbie. It's all decided. Any kind of dog you want. Just name it."

MY DOG, CAT

Uncle Jerry cleared his throat and muttered, "Doesn't need to be as expensive as that Chinese crested. A regular kind of dog would do."

"Oh, my word. That's so generous of you." Abbie's mom handed baby Lee back to Aunt Laura and hugged her, whispering something in her ear. She stepped back and took something out of her apron pocket and handed it to Aunt Laura. It looked like a tightly folded piece of paper.

Abbie's dad gingerly took the Chinese crested from Aunt Laura. "There you go, son," he encouraged, nudging Abbie while he held the strange new dog out at arm's length. "It looks like you're going to get the dog you've been wishing for. What do you say to that?"

"Great." Abbie's voice sounded weak. He tried to smile, but his cheeks felt stiff.

Aunt Laura looked up from the paper she held in her hands, a strange expression on her face.

"I thought you wanted a big dog named Killer?" she said softly, staring at Abbie.

"That *is* what he wants," said his dad. "It's what he's always wanted."

If I Had Three Wishes

But his mother was shaking her head. "Things change," she said. "Children grow up when we're not looking. Don't they, Laura?"

Aunt Laura cleared her throat and began to read out loud. It was a poem. A poem Abbie had written last week. A dumb old poem he'd crumpled up and tossed in the trash can. He must have missed and his mom had picked it up off the floor when she was vacuuming.

"Too many wishes just fall flat," Aunt Laura read. Abbie could feel his cheeks getting warm. Cat looked up, as if he could sense what Abbie was feeling, and licked his chin.

"Don't want some of this, don't want more
     of that,
Just wish I could call you my dog, Cat.

Wanted a "killer," big and strong,
but that was dumb and I was wrong.

Who knew that small is where it's at?
If I had three wishes, they'd all be Cat."

Aunt Laura finished and folded the paper without looking up. When she finally looked

MY DOG, CAT

at Abbie, her eyes were shining. "You really care about this little dog, don't you?"

"Huh?" Uncle Jerry looked questioningly from Aunt Laura to Abbie. "But I thought Abbie wanted a big dog? That's what everybody told me."

"Cat *is* big." Abbie said, and he could feel Cat's tail thump against his arm at the sound of his name. The dog rested in the crook of Abbie's elbow as if he'd grown there. As if he were a part of Abbie's body, like his arm or his leg—or his heart.

"Oh, Abbie," Aunt Laura whispered. "He looks so happy there." She bent down and rested a hand lightly on Cat's head, stroking the silky fur. "This really is a special little dog."

Uncle Jerry took Laura's hand and pulled her aside. "I know you were hoping that Cat could show Byrd the ropes, Laura," Abbie heard him say. "But what good is a dog who wants to be somewhere else? With some special boy." Aunt Laura and Uncle Jerry continued to talk, now in low voices. Finally they came back.

100

If I Had Three Wishes

"We said whatever dog you wanted, and we meant it," said Uncle Jerry.

Aunt Laura smiled at Abbie through moist eyes. "I love Cat, too, Abbie. But Jerry's right. He's made his home with you."

Uncle Jerry nodded. "And you can call him whatever you like, now that he's yours, son." He reached over and placed a big hand on Abbie's shoulder. "And he is yours, Ab. He's all yours."

The funny thing was, Uncle Jerry didn't look a bit like a fairy godmother. He wore a navy blue polo shirt, baggy khaki Bermuda shorts, and an orange-and-black Baltimore Orioles baseball cap. There was nothing gauzy or irridescent or magical about Uncle Jerry.

But Uncle Jerry had granted three wishes with one wave of his big hand.

Abbie had wished for a guy's name. Then Uncle Jerry called him Ab. Maybe other people had called him that before. But there was something about the man-to-man way Uncle Jerry said the name Ab. He'd had a guy's name all along. Even if people still called him Abbie, he didn't really mind. A name was what you made it, and not the other way around. Just look at Cat.

His wish to be tall hadn't exactly come true. But he felt bigger somehow. And one thing was sure: he was plenty tall enough to be Abbott Williamson the Third.

As for the big-black-dog wish, well, it was clear to Abbie now that any dog you love is automatically as big as you need it to be. What had Heather said at Arnie's? Something like, it's not the size of the dog in your heart, it's the size of the heart in your dog?

"I don't want to change your name," Abbie said softly, looking deep into Cat's dark eyes. "You'll always be Cat to me." The dog's gaze fastened adoringly on Abbie's face. Suddenly Cat gave one of those sharp, surprisingly deep-throated barks, and slurped his tongue across Abbie's nose and the bottom of his glasses.

"Quit it, Killer."

Everyone, including Marie, began to laugh and clap and reach out to pet the little Yorkie. Cat was busy licking inside Abbie's left ear, across to his eye, and down the side of his nose. Byrd was doing the same to Abbie's dad.

Abbie smiled. He wouldn't bother cleaning his glasses yet. Not until Cat was done. He settled down to let the dog's tongue do its work while he thought about the three new wishes he had to plan. He was sure there still must be things he wanted.

Funny thing was, right this minute, with Cat in his arms, he couldn't seem to think of a single thing he didn't already have.

Afterword:
The Dog in
Your Heart

It's amazing but true.

There are more than four hundred breeds of dog recognized by kennel clubs in dozens of countries around the world.

All of them originated from *Tomarctus*, a badgerlike ancestor of both wolves and bears. It was six million years ago that *Tomarctus* gave rise to the genus *Canis*, and for the past twenty thousand years, people have been shaping and reshaping the dog to be and do whatever best suits human needs.

Besides the purebred dogs, there are also endless mixed breeds, affectionately known as mutts, with qualities as varied as their looks.

The Dog in Your Heart

Picking the right dog is like picking a best friend. It's part what you have in common, part something magical you feel inside, and part knowing you can depend on this significant other to listen, to share, and never to judge you no matter what. There is a right dog for everybody who wants one—often more than one.

You just have to decide what you like.

Some dogs are small (like Cat, a Yorkshire terrier), others big (like Great Danes), fast (greyhounds), slow (basset hounds), abundant (German shepherds) or rare (Tahltan bear dogs). Some are rambunctious (Dalmatians), some drool (Saint Bernards), and some are prone to special problems (like skin rashes in shar-peis and back problems in dachshunds). These are good things to know before you and your parents make a decision about the right dog for you.

One of the best ways to make up your mind is to read about dogs in interesting reference books such as *The Complete Dog Book for Kids* by the American Kennel Club (New York: Howell Books, 1996), *Dog* by Juliet Clutton-Brock

MY DOG, CAT

(New York: Alfred A. Knopf, 1991), and *Dogs* by Amanda O'Neill (New York: Kingfisher, 1999).

But before you choose a dog, visit both kennels and shelters to meet a few possibilities in person. Like Abbie, the dog you *think* you want may not always match the dog you fall in love with.